J
977.8
La

$12.95

LaDoux, Rita C
      Missouri

DATE DUE

JA 31 01		
AG 19 02		
FE 25		

MISSOURI

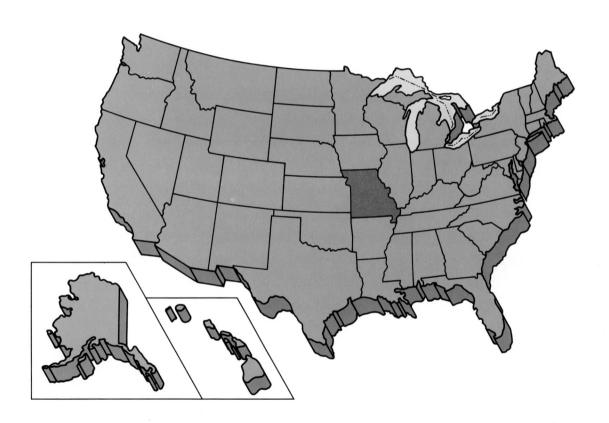

Hello U★S★A★

MISSOURI

Rita C. LaDoux

Lerner Publications Company

LIBRARY OF CONGRESS
CATALOGING-IN-PUBLICATION DATA
LaDoux, Rita.
    Missouri / Rita C. LaDoux
        p.   cm. — (Hello USA)
    Includes index.
    Summary: Introduces the geography, history, people, industries, and other highlights of Missouri.
    ISBN 0-8225-2710-3 (lib. bdg.)
    1. Missouri—Juvenile literature.
    [1. Missouri.] I. Title. II. Series.
    F466.3.L33 1991
    977.8—dc20   90-13529
                                        CIP
                                        AC

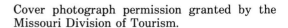

Cover photograph permission granted by the Missouri Division of Tourism.

The glossary that begins on page 68 gives definitions of words shown in **bold type** in the text.

Manufactured in the United States of America
1 2 3 4 5 6 7 8 9 10 99 98 97 96 95 94 93 92 91

This book is printed on acid-free, recyclable paper.

CONTENTS

Did You Know . . . ?

❑ America's first daylight bank robbery occurred on February 13, 1866, in Liberty, Missouri. Bandits stole more than $60,000 from the Clay County Savings Bank and Loan Association. The case was never solved, but many people believe Jesse James staged the robbery.

❑ Missouri takes its name from the Missouri River. The name may mean "muddy water" or "people of the large canoes" in the language of the Missouri Indians.

World's Fair, 1904

❑ The first people to taste hot dogs and ice cream cones were visitors at the St. Louis World's Fair in 1904.

❑ Lake of the Ozarks in central Missouri has a shoreline that runs 1,375 miles (2,212 kilometers). That's longer than the Pacific coast of California!

❑ Early traders floated furs down Missouri's rivers in crafts called bull boats. The boats were made of willow saplings covered with buffalo hides. Only male, or bull, skins were used because female hides leaked too easily.

A Trip Around the State

"Away, we're bound away, 'cross the wide Missouri," sang wistful travelers as they headed for the river nicknamed Big Muddy. The two longest rivers in the United States, the Missouri and the Mississippi, meet in the state of Missouri. These rivers made Missouri a gateway to the West—a place where pioneers began their westward travels.

9

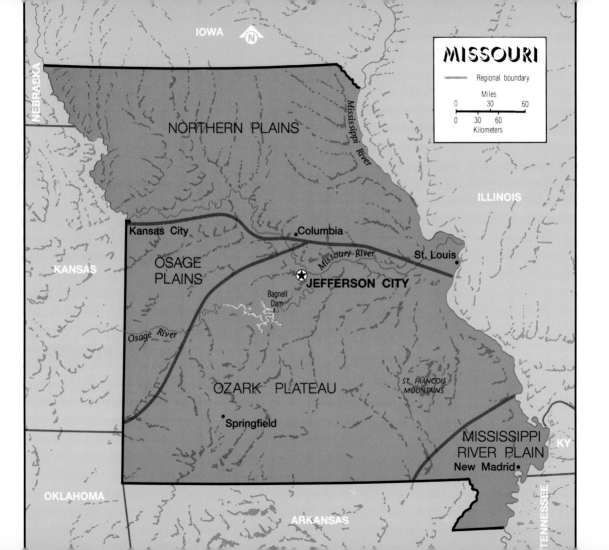

IOWA

N

MISSOURI

Regional boundary

Miles
0   30   60

0   30   60
Kilometers

NEBRASKA

NORTHERN PLAINS

Mississippi River

ILLINOIS

• Kansas City

• Columbia

St. Louis •

KANSAS

OSAGE
PLAINS

Missouri River

★ JEFFERSON CITY

Bagnell
Dam

Osage River

OZARK   PLATEAU

ST. FRANCOIS
MOUNTAINS

• Springfield

MISSISSIPPI
RIVER PLAIN

KY

New Madrid •

OKLAHOMA

TENNESSEE

ARKANSAS

Missouri is surrounded by eight other states. To the east of the Mississippi River lie Illinois, Kentucky, and Tennessee. Other boundaries are formed by Arkansas, Oklahoma, Kansas, Nebraska, and Iowa. Only one other state, Tennessee, has as many neighbors.

Missouri has four geographic regions—the Northern Plains, the Osage Plains, the Ozark Plateau, and the Mississippi River Plain. During the **Ice Age** hundreds of thousands of years ago, **glaciers** moved into the Northern Plains. The huge, thick sheets of ice crept over the land, grinding up rocks and plants. In their path, the glaciers left rich soil and sand.

Streams wore through the dirt, carving hills in the Northern Plains. Forests grew in the eastern part of this region. Tall grasses sprouted over the western hills and the Osage Plains, the region in west central Missouri. Centuries of decaying grasses have made the flat **prairies** (grasslands) of the Osage Plains quite fertile.

Pale purple coneflowers add splashes of color to the prairies of western Missouri.

11

The rolling hills of the Ozark Plateau stretch as far as the eye can see.

Wooded hills and mountains blanket the Ozark Plateau, which covers most of southern Missouri. Millions of years ago, pressures deep underground pushed this region above the surrounding land, creating a **plateau,** or tableland. Rivers have since worn deep gorges into the plateau. The St. Francois Mountains, the tallest in the state, stand in the southeastern part of the Ozark Plateau.

Visitors marvel at the underground wonders in Meramec Caverns and other caves.

Mysterious sights hide beneath the surface of the Ozark Plateau. Water seeping down through the soil and bubbling up from underground springs has carved huge caves in the soft limestone. Icicle-like formations fascinate those who visit the caverns.

To the southeast, along the Mississippi River, sprawls the Mississippi River Plain. Called the Boot Heel because of its shape, this low flat plain was once a great **swamp,** or wetland. Farmers have drained the swamp to turn it into cropland.

When the Mississippi River rolls past the Boot Heel, it is much wider and deeper than it is when it first enters the state. Some of the river's largest **tributaries**—the Missouri, Illinois, and Ohio rivers—enter the Mississippi at points along Missouri's eastern border. These waters add to the Mississippi River, making it much bigger.

Not all of Missouri's water makes its way to the Mississippi. Workers have dammed, or blocked, some rivers, especially on the Ozark Plateau. The backed-up waters have created the state's only large lakes. People enjoy swimming and fishing in the lakes, but they were built mainly to control floods and to supply **hydroelectric power.** Water flowing through the dams turns engines that create electricity.

Water also affects Missouri's weather. Farther down the Mississippi, moist air rises from the waters of the Gulf of Mexico, keeping most of Missouri humid and warm in the summer. Winter brings occasional snowfalls that range from 8 to 20 inches (20 to 51 centimeters). But in Missouri's mild climate, snow usually melts in less than a week.

Bagnell Dam on the Osage River backs up water for 130 miles (209 kilometers) to form Lake of the Ozarks.

The warm air that originates in the Gulf of Mexico can become dangerous. Tornadoes form with little warning during spring and summer thunderstorms. Twisters whirl across the state, leaving behind trails of flattened barns and uprooted trees.

Earthquakes also occasionally rock Missouri. In 1811 a major quake hit New Madrid, in the state's southeastern corner. Scientists predict that another major tremor will strike the state.

But overall, Missouri's weather is gentle enough to allow many plants and animals to thrive. One-third of the state is covered with stands of hardwood trees. Oak, hickory, and walnut trees provide

Hikers enjoy the state's parks and forests.

16

food for the white-tailed deer and wild turkeys that live in the lush forests.

Bobwhite quail feast on seeds along grassy borders of the woodlands. And beavers, nature's dam builders, create small ponds along Missouri's streams.

Cave salamanders make their homes in Missouri's damp, dark caverns.

Missouri's Story

Rivers have long been used as highways, and many people followed them to the land that would become Missouri. The first of these people arrived more than 10,000 years ago. These Indians, or Native Americans, lived in caves and ate the nuts, berries, and plants that they gathered. They hunted small and large animals, including mastodons—huge elephants that roamed North America after the last Ice Age.

Later, people who lived in the area learned to grow corn, beans, and squash. One Indian tribe, the Missouri, built villages on bluffs that overlooked the Missouri River.

Around A.D. 700 another group, the Mississippi Mound Builders, settled along the Mississippi River. These Indians became skilled farmers. They raised enough crops to feed people living in large villages. Cahokia, near what is now St. Louis, was the largest Mississippian community.

The Indians at Cahokia built temple mounds for religious ceremonies. The central community was surrounded by outlying villages and fields.

Many Osage men were over six feet (1.8 meters) tall. They shaved their eyebrows and heads, leaving only a small patch of hair on top of their heads.

By 1500 more than 30,000 Indians lived in Cahokia. Its location on the Mississippi River made it a trading center. Indians came to Cahokia to sell grizzly-bear teeth from the Rocky Mountains, seashells from the Gulf of Mexico, and copper from what is now Minnesota.

In the 1600s, the lives of both the Mississippian and Missouri Indians were destroyed. Although European explorers had not yet reached Missouri, their diseases had. Unaware that they were infecting others, traveling Indians who had been exposed to sick people from other tribes carried the diseases from village to village. By the late 1600s, many Mississippian and Missouri Indians had died, and the rest had fled their villages to escape illness.

Other tribes moved onto land abandoned by the Mississippian and Missouri Indians. From the east came the Kansa, Illinois, and Osage. The Osage built five villages on tributaries of the

Missouri River. Farmers and hunters, the Osage also raided neighboring tribes for food and slaves.

Meanwhile, European explorers had reached Missouri. Two Frenchmen, Jacques Marquette and Louis Jolliet, paddled canoes down the Mississippi River in 1673. In a diary of his travels, Marquette wrote that he was amazed at the huge, muddy river—the Missouri—that rushed into the Mississippi.

As they explored the Missouri area, Marquette and Jolliet met Oto, Missouri, and Osage Indians.

In 1682 Sieur de La Salle claimed for France the Mississippi and all the rivers that flowed into it. This vast piece of land stretched west from the Appalachians to the Rocky Mountains and south from Canada to the Gulf of Mexico. La Salle named the area Louisiana after the French king Louis XIV.

The first French settlers in the part of Louisiana that is now Missouri named their village Sainte Genevieve. Indians brought pelts to the riverside village to trade for blankets, mirrors, horses, guns, and liquor. By 1727 French miners were shipping lead from Sainte Genevieve all the way to New Orleans.

In 1764, 15-year-old René Auguste Chouteau traveled up the Mississippi River from New Orleans with his stepfather, Pierre Laclède. Just south of where the Missouri and Mississippi rivers meet, the men built a fur-trading post called Laclède's Landing. They bought pelts from the Osage Indians. The fur trade thrived, and Laclède's Landing quickly grew into a busy French settlement—St. Louis.

At riverside trading posts, Indians exchanged furs for goods such as tobacco, buckshot, and glass beads.

23

After founding St. Louis, René Auguste Chouteau and his family built a fur-trading empire.

For years the Chouteau family and the Osage trappers controlled the fur trade along the Missouri River. But life in the region began to change rapidly after 1803, when the United States bought all of Louisiana from France in a deal called the Louisiana Purchase.

Thomas Jefferson, the U.S. president, sent explorers Meriwether Lewis and William Clark to map the territory and to find a river route to the Pacific Ocean. Jefferson believed their discoveries would allow the United States to spread from the Atlantic to the Pacific coast. In 1804 the explorers left from St. Louis and steered their boats up the Missouri River.

24

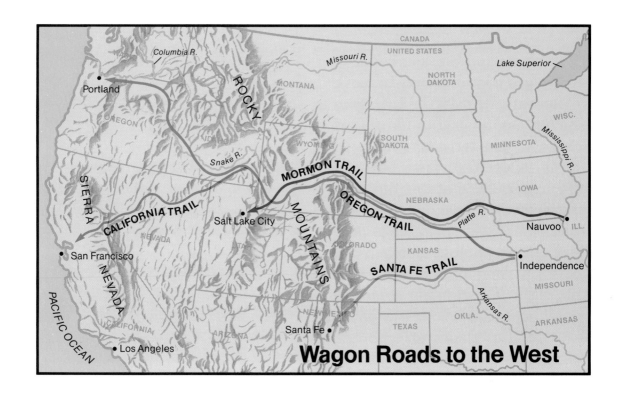

The expedition lasted more than two years. Part of the route Lewis and Clark mapped later became the Oregon Trail, a wagon-train road that began in Missouri and ended on the West Coast.

The Lewis and Clark expedition encouraged a lot of people to move to Missouri. In 1812 the U.S. government established the Missouri Territory. As a territory, Missouri had to follow U.S. laws but had fewer rights than states did.

River trade expanded. In 1817 crowds gathered to watch a paddle-wheel steamboat dock in St. Louis's harbor for the first time. Able to carry large loads, steamers would soon replace the smaller boats in use. Pilots steered the steamboats up the Missouri River to fur-trading posts as far away as Montana.

As more and more people traveled the rivers, Missouri's population grew. Missouri had attracted

Among Missouri's early settlers was Daniel Boone, the famous woodsman and pioneer. Boone found "elbow room" in Missouri in 1799, when he led a group of settlers from Kentucky to the uncharted land.

Steamboats traveled the rivers carrying everything from settlers and tools to gamblers and circuses. Mark Twain, one of Missouri's most famous riverboat pilots, wrote the book *Life on the Mississippi* based on his experiences on the river.

not only the French but also other pioneers. Many American Southerners moved into the area. With them they brought black slaves. Before long, nearly one out of every six people in the territory was a slave. Most were forced to work the land.

Pioneers packed saws, farming tools, needles, seeds, and salt into covered wagons *(left).* They tried to carry with them everything that they would need as they built new homes—such as this simple log cabin *(facing page)*—on the western frontier.

Pioneers built towns and farms throughout Missouri. The Indians in Missouri, however, were not happy about the change. Gradually, their hunting grounds shrank as white settlers plowed fields for corn and wheat. With less land, the Indians could no longer live as their ancestors had. At first, the tribes fought to defend their lands from settlers. But eventually, Indians in Missouri gave up their territory and moved farther west.

Missouri's state flag was adopted in 1913. The ring of stars represents Missouri's entry into the Union as the 24th state.

In the early 1800s, the territory had ample land, settlers, crops, and furs. Yet Missourians yearned for something more. In 1818 they asked the U.S. government to make their territory a state. But there was one problem.

Missourians who had come from the South wanted to keep their slaves. Many Americans, however, believed that slavery was wrong. Members of the U.S. Congress tried to keep the number of states that allowed slavery (slave states) equal to the number of states that did not allow slavery (free states).

If Missouri entered the Union as a slave state, there would be more slave states than free states. Missouri's request for statehood was delayed for two years, until Maine asked to enter the Union as a free state. To accept the two states, members of Congress struck a deal called the **Missouri Compromise**. On August 10, 1821, Missouri became the 24th state, a slave state.

The same year, a trader named William Becknell traced the Santa Fe Trail. This route followed an old Indian trail. It led 780 miles (1,255 km) west from Independence, Missouri, to the city of Santa Fe in territory owned by Mexico.

In Santa Fe, traders from Missouri exchanged manufactured goods for silver and mules. This trade made some Missourians rich and gave the state one of its nicknames, the Mule State.

Mules hauled many of the covered wagons on the Oregon and Santa Fe trails.

St. Louis's waterfront exploded in a mass of flames in 1849, when a fire ravaged the port. The blaze destroyed 23 steamboats and over $5 million worth of property.

Merchants in St. Louis grew rich selling supplies to the pioneers. Almost every day, steamboats packed with people, food, and tools left the city for Independence and posts farther up the Missouri River. Steamers chugged back down the river loaded with furs and sometimes with gold.

As more and more pioneers settled lands west of the Mississippi, U.S. citizens argued about whether to allow slavery in these new territories. The slave states in the South and the free states in the North could not settle their disagreements about slavery and other issues. In 1861 the Civil War broke out between the North and the South.

33

The Dred Scott Decision

Dred Scott was a slave who lived in Missouri during the early 1800s. Scott's fight for freedom came to represent the fight over slavery.

As an adult, Scott moved around with his owner to states that did not allow slavery. When his owner died in Missouri, a slave state, Scott believed he should become a free man. He had, after all, lived in free states. Scott sued his master's widow for his freedom in 1846.

The trial for Scott's case was heard first by the Missouri Supreme Court in St. Louis and then by the U.S. Supreme Court. Both courts agreed that Scott was still a slave.

In 1857 the U.S. Supreme Court ruled in the Dred Scott decision that black people were not U.S. citizens, and so they could not use the nation's court system. The Court also ruled that Congress could not ban slavery in U.S. territories.

After the Supreme Court made its decision, Scott was sold to a new owner, who freed the slave. But the Court's ruling against Scott made many people angry. The Dred Scott decision gave Northerners and Southerners one more reason to begin the Civil War.

During the Civil War, Union soldiers dug a channel through a swamp along the Mississippi River near New Madrid. This path allowed them to sneak a transport boat past a Confederate camp on one of the river's islands.

Most Missourians wanted their state to remain in the Union. But some of Missouri's leaders thought the state should join the Confederacy (a separate government formed by the Southern states). Missouri's governor, Claiborne Jackson, acted against the wishes of most Missourians when he commanded Missouri's troops to fight Union soldiers. The Union quickly gained control of northern Missouri.

Jackson and his supporters continued to operate out of southwestern Missouri, fighting a major battle at Wilson's Creek. After

This Civil War cannon at Wilson's Creek reminds visitors of the 2,500 soldiers who died in the battle there in 1861.

Jackson was defeated in 1862, **bushwhackers** and **jayhawkers** continued the violence. These opposing groups—bushwhackers supported the South and jayhawkers sided with the North—raided farms and towns and killed many people.

In 1865 the South surrendered, and the Civil War finally ended. But Missouri and the West were no longer the same. The war had ended slavery, and other changes also took place. Railroads were built across the country, and trains began moving goods once ferried on rivers or carried over wagon trails. Steamboats, the former queens of the river, sat unused in their ports.

The whistle of steam locomotives announced the arrival of beef from Kansas City, Missouri, or manufactured goods from St. Louis. By the late 1800s, railroads linked towns and cities across the United States.

At the World's Fair held in St. Louis, countries from around the world displayed the most modern technologies of 1904.

Though Missouri had lost some of its allure as an untamed land, its appeal was still strong. The state continued to grow, and its cities became important industrial and agricultural centers.

During World War I (1914–1918), aging steamers went back to work. They pushed barges loaded with food and manufactured goods down the Mississippi River to New Orleans. There, Missouri's products were loaded onto ships bound for Europe. River trade flourished again.

How Missouri Framed Jesse James

Jesse James and his gang rob a train in this section of a mural painted by Thomas Hart Benton. Like several other bandits, James began robbing and killing as a bushwhacker during the Civil War. Before he was shot in 1882, James staged about 25 robberies.

Benton painted the mural on the walls of the state capitol in Jefferson City during the 1930s. Benton had captured the spirit of his native Missouri, but state lawmakers were outraged because he had not painted heroes and politicians. Instead, he illustrated the rascals and common people of the state—ruthless train robbers, dishonest fur traders, hardworking women, and escaping slaves.

10,000 B.C.　　**A.D. 700**　　**1673**　　　　　　　　　　　　　　　**1764**　　　　　　　**1803**

Early Indians hunt
mastodons in the area
now called Missouri

Indians settle in villages
along the Mississippi River

Marquette and Jolliet explore the Mississippi River

Chouteau and Laclède
build a fur-trading outpost
near present-day St. Louis

Louisiana Purchase

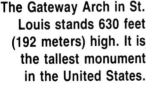

The Gateway Arch in St.
Louis stands 630 feet
(192 meters) high. It is
the tallest monument
in the United States.

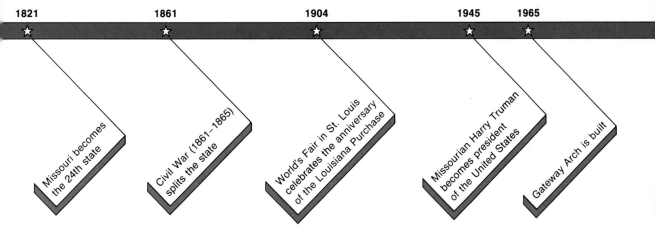

1821	1861	1904	1945	1965

Missouri becomes the 24th state

Civil War (1861–1865) splits the state

World's Fair in St. Louis celebrates the anniversary of the Louisiana Purchase

Missourian Harry Truman becomes president of the United States

Gateway Arch is built

Missouri continued to develop industries throughout the 1900s. During World War II (1939–1945), the state's factories made supplies for the U.S. Army. Near the end of the war, Missourian Harry S. Truman became president of the United States.

In 1965 the Gateway Arch was built in St. Louis as a reminder of Missouri's role as the Gateway to the West. From the top of the arch, viewers can see barges trailing the Mississippi. To the west lies the land opened by hardworking traders, miners, and farmers. Each pioneer who came to Missouri followed a dream—a dream of a better life on America's western frontier.

Holiday lights brighten stores in Kansas City.

Living and Working in Missouri

In 1899 a Missouri congressman claimed that fancy speeches did not impress him. He said, "I am from Missouri. You have got to show me." Since then, people have called Missouri the Show Me State.

Nearly 5.2 million people live in the Show Me State. Seven out of every ten Missourians make their home in the state's cities. Major cities include St. Louis, Kansas City, Columbia, Independence, Joplin, and Springfield. The state's capital, Jefferson City, was named for President Thomas Jefferson.

Most Missourians were born in the United States. Almost 90 percent have ancestors from European countries such as France, England, Germany, Czechoslovakia, Italy, and Ireland. People with African ancestors make up about 10 percent of the state's population. Smaller numbers of Missourians are Hispanic, Asian, or American Indian.

Each summer, the people of Sainte Genevieve celebrate their French heritage during Jour de Fete *(right).* And at historical parks, students learn how ancient Indians ground corn *(below).*

44

Museums and historic sites throughout the state give visitors a peek into Missouri's past. Some of the area's oldest artworks are preserved at Washington State Park, where pictures of animals were carved into stone by Indians about 1,000 years ago.

The lives of Jesse James, George Washington Carver, Daniel Boone, and other people from the state's past are featured at historical exhibits. Missouri's history is also represented at the Harry S. Truman Library in Independence and on murals at the state capitol building in Jefferson City.

Dance, musicals, and plays entertain city audiences, while action-packed historical shows please crowds at vacation-area theaters. Missouri's musicians perform country, blues, jazz, and classical music.

Neatness is not important at Hannibal's annual Tom Sawyer Fence Painting Contest.

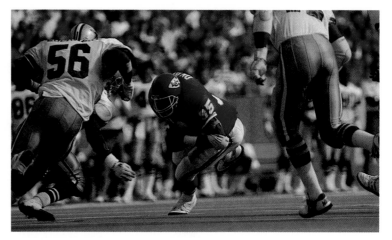
Kansas City Chiefs

St. Louis Cardinals

No matter what the season, Missouri has a professional sports team in action. All winter, the Kansas City Blades and the St. Louis Blues skate for hockey honors. The Kansas City Comets and the St. Louis Storm keep indoor soccer fans cheering.

Spring and summer bring out baseball fans wearing blue for the Kansas City Royals or red

Missourians enjoy casting for fish in the state's lakes and rivers.

for the St. Louis Cardinals. As fall approaches, the Kansas City Chiefs warm up to play football.

Outdoor Missouri offers fun for everyone. Real snow melts quickly in Missouri, but winter skiers enjoy gliding down slopes covered with machine-made snow. Canoeing and river rafting are popular summer activities. And each year millions of vacationers visit the state's parks and lakes.

Workers assemble vans in St. Louis.

Missouri's recreational opportunities make living and working in the state attractive to many people. Over half of the Missourians who work have service jobs. Workers in service jobs help other people or businesses. These workers include teachers, doctors, salespeople, and car mechanics.

Many service workers earn their living helping others enjoy their stay in Missouri. Some operate resorts on lakes and rivers. Rangers welcome campers at the state and national parks. Food servers, hotel clerks, and entertainers also help make tourism one of Missouri's most important businesses.

About 20 percent of Missouri's workers hold jobs in factories. Most of these people have jobs in the St. Louis and Kansas City areas. Some factory workers tend machines that produce chemicals for farms and industries. Others may be skilled mechanics who build cars, truck bodies, railroad cars, barges, or airplanes.

Missouri's river highways and the state's history as a trading center led to another major industry—transportation. St. Louis and Kansas City are hubs for truck, railroad, airline, and river barge traffic. Many products are shipped by barge from St. Louis to other U.S. ports. And the grain loaded in St. Louis or Kansas City may end up almost anywhere in the world.

Kansas City has been a meat-packing and flour-milling town ever since workers built a railroad bridge across the Missouri River in 1869. From the country's western plains, trains transport cattle and wheat across the bridge to Kansas City.

Meat-processing plants in Missouri butcher cows and pigs. Kansas City's mills rank second in the nation for grinding wheat into flour.

Missouri's pigs feed on corn and other grains grown in the state.

Soybeans are Missouri's most important crop.

Farmers in the state grow many crops. On the prairies and rolling hills in northern and central Missouri, farmers plant soybeans and corn. The Mississippi River Plain provides rich soil for growing cotton and rice. The hilly lands of the Ozark Plateau are difficult to farm, but the area is good for grazing beef and dairy cattle and for growing wheat.

51

Coal strip-mined in Missouri is burned at nearby power plants to produce electricity.

A few of Missouri's workers are keeping some old traditions alive. Lead, which was mined by Missouri's first French settlers, is still found in large quantities in the state's southern counties. Missouri produces more lead than any other state. Workers also mine coal and iron from the Ozark hills.

German settlers came to the Hermann area in central Missouri because it reminded them of the grape-growing valleys of Germany. Hermann's wine makers still crush grapes to make wine. Another German tradition—beer making—is followed at the Anheuser-Busch brewery in St. Louis. And, as a clear reminder of pioneer days, Missouri is still the nation's top breeder of mules.

Bands entertain tourists with German polkas at Hermann's Maifest.

Protecting the Environment

For the Indians who once lived in the area, Missouri was a land of plenty. Huge herds of buffalo grazed on the grassy plains. Deer and wild turkeys roamed the forests. And the rivers were swimming with catfish, beavers, and otters. Each spring and fall, migrating ducks and geese filled the skies.

When the French trappers arrived, life became more difficult for Missouri's wildlife. The trappers killed many animals for their furs. Then settlers began clearing the woodlands and prairies to make room for crops. Later, hunters killed birds by the hundreds and shipped them to restaurants on the East Coast, where menus featured wild quail and duck.

By the late 1920s, hunters had killed all the buffalo, deer, and wild turkeys in the state. Then came the Great Depression. Many people lost their jobs. They hunted wild animals to feed their families. Within 10 years, nearly all of Missouri's game animals were gone.

The disappearance of animals troubled many Missourians. In 1937 Missouri became the first state to start a department of conservation. This new government office planned to base its hunting and fishing rules on research about animals.

Since the Department of Conservation was formed, scientists have studied the types of food and shelter needed by different plants and animals. Researchers also find out how animals raise their young. The department uses this information to help plant and animal populations survive and grow.

Many organizations have helped Missouri's Department of Conservation protect the habitats of various animals. By buying and preserving areas in the state that provide natural habitats, these groups make certain that wild animals will be able to find the food and shelter they need.

Bald cypress trees tower over the swamp at Mingo National Wildlife Refuge. These and other government-owned lands provide havens for Missouri's wild animals.

**White-tailed deer
listen for hunters.**

River otters fish in Missouri's streams.

An early success came at the end of the 1930s. The state government brought a few deer back into the state, then banned deer hunting. In the following years, the deer raised many fawns. Slowly, the number of these animals began to rise. Once the deer population became large enough, limited hunting was allowed.

Wildlife scientists have brought back other animals that had disappeared from the state. Not long ago, all the state's wild turkeys, bald eagles, Canada geese, trumpeter swans, ruffed grouse, and river otters were gone. Because of successful wildlife programs, all of these animals are again thriving and raising young in Missouri.

Although some animals can now be hunted without harming their populations, others, such as the prairie chicken, may never be hunted again. Most of this bird's habitat—prairie—has been planted with crops. Missouri will probably never again have enough natural grassland to support a large number of prairie chickens.

Prairie chickens dance to attract mates.

Missouri's hunters help protect the size of animal populations in the state by following laws that control the number of animals killed each year.

All Missourians contribute to the state's wildlife programs. In 1976 the people of the state voted to raise taxes to help fund the Department of Conservation. Many residents also give money to private wildlife organizations. And volunteers help teach people about animals and their habitats.

Huge herds of buffalo may never again thunder across Missouri's plains. But nature lovers can watch for the flight of a bald eagle, the leap of a deer, and the splash of a beaver's tail. By working together, Missourians have maintained a home for wildlife in their state.

Missouri's Famous People

◀ **ED ASNER**

ACTORS

Ed Asner (born 1929) worked on his first newspaper in high school in Kansas City, Missouri. He became known to television viewers as newsman Lou Grant on both "The Mary Tyler Moore Show" and "Lou Grant."

Kathleen Turner (born 1954) grew up in Springfield, Missouri. An actress, Turner has starred in many movies, including *Romancing the Stone*, *The Accidental Tourist*, and *War of the Roses*.

KATHLEEN TURNER ▶

THOMAS HART BENTON ▶

ARTISTS

Thomas Hart Benton (1889–1975), who was named after his great-uncle the politician, was born in Neosho, Missouri. Benton painted scenes of American life in the Midwest and South. His murals are known for their strong lines and bright colors.

George Caleb Bingham (1811–1879) lived in Missouri from the time he was eight years old. He made his living painting portraits, but he is remembered for his scenes of frontier life.

Walt Disney (1901–1966) grew up in Marceline and in Kansas City, Missouri. Disney pioneered the use of animation in movies. His cartoon characters Mickey Mouse, Donald Duck, and Cinderella are known around the world. Disney also produced nature films and television programs and built Disneyland and Disney World.

▲ **WALT DISNEY**

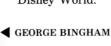

◀ **GEORGE BINGHAM**

ATHLETES

Lawrence ("Yogi") Berra (born 1925), a native of St. Louis, was a catcher for the Yankees from 1946 to 1963. He holds the record for playing in the most (14) World Series. In 1965 Berra began coaching for the New York Mets, and in 1972 he became manager of that team. Berra is also known for his love of comic books.

Michael Spinks (born 1956) is a champion boxer who grew up in St. Louis. Spinks gained fans all across the United States when he and his brother Leon each won gold medals in boxing at the 1976 Olympic Games.

YOGI BERRA ▶

◀ ADOLPHUS BUSCH

J. C. PENNEY ▶

BUSINESS LEADERS

Adolphus Busch (1839–1913) emigrated from Germany to St. Louis and married the daughter of a beer brewer named Anheuser. Later, Busch became president of Anheuser's company and renamed it Anheuser-Busch. Busch was among the first to pasteurize beer. This process made it possible to ship beer long distances without refrigeration.

James Cash Penney (1875–1971), a native of Hamilton, Missouri, founded the J. C. Penney department-store chain. In 1902 he opened his first general store, called the Golden Rule. At the time of Penney's death in 1971, his company had 1,640 stores and sales had topped $4.8 billion.

MUSICIANS

Chuck Berry (born 1926) is a guitarist and singer who helped change the sound of popular American music. Berry started out playing blues music in St. Louis, his hometown. His real success came when he began playing rock and roll in the late 1950s. Berry's hits include "Roll Over Beethoven," "Sweet Little Sixteen," "Rock and Roll Music," and "Johnny B. Goode."

Scott Joplin (1868–1917) settled in Sedalia, Missouri, in 1896. There he developed his own style of jazz piano, called ragtime. His best-known tunes include "Maple Leaf Rag" and "The Entertainer."

◀ CHUCK BERRY

SCOTT JOPLIN ▶

◀ HARRY TRUMAN

ROY WILKINS ▶

POLITICAL LEADERS

Thomas Hart Benton (1782–1858) represented Missouri in the U.S. Senate for 30 years (1821–1851). He was strongly in favor of expanding the United States west across North America.

Harry S. Truman (1884–1972) grew up in Independence, Missouri. In 1944 President Franklin Roosevelt chose Truman to run for the office of vice-president of the United States. Just 83 days after being sworn into office, Roosevelt died and Truman became president. He served as president from 1945 to 1953.

Roy Wilkins (1901–1981) was born in St. Louis. From 1955 to 1977 he served as executive secretary for the National Association for the Advancement of Colored People (NAACP). He was known for his thoughtful leadership and for using the court system to protect the rights of black people.

64

George Washington Carver (1864–1943) was born near Diamond, Missouri. As a boy, Carver was interested in plants, a fascination that led him to become a leading agricultural scientist. He is best known for products that he created from peanuts, including meal, ink, linoleum, and plastics.

Edwin Powell Hubble (1889–1953), born in Marshfield, Missouri, was an astronomer who changed the way we look at the universe. By studying stars through a large telescope, Hubble proved that many other galaxies lie far outside our Milky Way. The first space telescope, which the United States launched in 1990, is named for Hubble.

▲ GEORGE WASHINGTON CARVER

MARK TWAIN ▶

WRITERS

Langston Hughes (1902–1967), a native of Joplin, Missouri, used street language and the musical rhythms of the blues to write about the lives of black people. His works include *Weary Blues, Not Without Laughter,* and *The Ways of White Folks.*

Mark Twain (1835–1910) is the pen name used by Samuel Clemens, who grew up in Hannibal, Missouri. Twain developed an American style of writing using the everyday speech he had heard in Hannibal. Two of his best-known books are *The Adventures of Tom Sawyer* and *Adventures of Huckleberry Finn.*

Laura Ingalls Wilder (1867–1957) settled in Mansfield, Missouri, in 1894. There, at the age of 60, she began to write a children's series called the "Little House" books. These stories describe Wilder's childhood on the plains of the Midwest.

▲ LANGSTON HUGHES

◀ LAURA INGALLS WILDER

Facts-at-a-Glance

Nickname: Show Me State
Song: "Missouri Waltz"
Motto: *Salus populi suprema lex esto*
   (The welfare of the people
   shall be the supreme law)
Flower: hawthorn
Tree: flowering dogwood
Bird: bluebird

Population: 5,192,000 (1990 estimate)
Rank in population, nationwide: 15th
Area: 69,697 sq mi (180,515 sq km)
Rank in area, nationwide: 19th
Date and ranking of statehood:
   August 10, 1821, the 24th state
Capital: Jefferson City (36,210*)
Major cities (and populations*):
   St. Louis (426,300), Kansas City (441,170),
   Springfield (139,360), Independence (112,950),
   St. Joseph (74,070), Columbia (63,140)
U.S. representatives: 9
U.S. senators: 2
Electoral votes: 11

*1986 estimates

Places to visit: Gateway Arch in St. Louis, Mark Twain Home and Museum near Hannibal, Meramec Caverns near Sullivan, Missouri Botanical Garden in St. Louis, Silver Dollar City near Branson

Annual Events: Ragtime Festival in St. Louis (June), Tom Sawyer Fence Painting Contest in Hannibal (July), Boot Heel Rodeo in Sikeston (Aug.), Jour de Fete in Sainte Genevieve (Aug.), Octoberfest in Hermann (Oct.)

Average January Temperature: 30° F (–1° C)   **Average July Temperature:** 78° F (26° C)

Natural resources: forests, fertile soil, water, lead, clay, stone, coal, iron ore, zinc

Agricultural products: soybeans, corn, wheat, hay, cotton, rice, popcorn, dairy cattle, beef cattle, eggs, chickens, turkeys, pigs, sheep, horses, mules

Manufactured goods: airplanes, barges, railroad cars, automobiles, truck and bus bodies, chemicals, machinery, paper and printed materials, steel

ENDANGERED SPECIES
Mammals—Indiana bat, eastern cougar, gray bat, Ozark big-eared bat
Birds—American peregrine falcon, bald eagle, Bachman's warbler, interior least tern
Fish and shellfish—Ozark cavefish, Niangua darter, Higgins's eye pearly mussel, pink mucket pearly mussel, Curtis's pearly mussel, fat pocketbook
Plants—large-flowered skullcap, pondberry, Missouri bladderpod

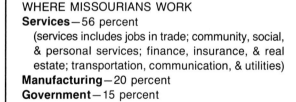

WHERE MISSOURIANS WORK
Services—56 percent
  (services includes jobs in trade; community, social, & personal services; finance, insurance, & real estate; transportation, communication, & utilities)
Manufacturing—20 percent
Government—15 percent
Agriculture—5 percent
Construction—4 percent

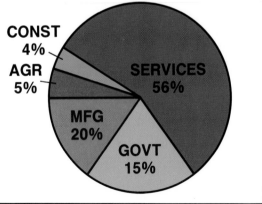

67

PRONUNCIATION GUIDE

Anheuser-Busch (AN-hy-sur BUSH)

Chouteau, René Auguste
  (shoo-TOH, reh-NAY oh-GOOST)

Jolliet, Louis (JOH-lee-eht, LOO-ihs)

Laclède, Pierre (lah-KLEHD, pee-AIR)

La Salle, Sieur de (luh SAL, syuh duh)

Marquette, Jacques
  (mahr-KEHT, zhahk)

New Orleans (noo OR-lee-uhns)

Osage (oh-SAYJ)

Ozark Plateau (OH-zahrk pla-TOH)

Sainte Genevieve
  (saynt JEHN-uh-veev)

Saint Francois (saynt FRAYNt-suhs)

Glossary

bushwhacker Someone who attacks others from a position of hiding. During the Civil War, bushwhackers were Confederate soldiers who worked independently, raiding and destroying the property of people who supported the Union.

glacier A large body of ice and snow that moves slowly over land.

hydroelectric power The electricity produced by using waterpower. Also called hydropower.

ice age A period when ice sheets cover large regions of the earth. The term *Ice Age* usually refers to the most recent one, called the Pleistocene, which began almost 2 million years ago and ended about 10,000 years ago.

jayhawker A member of a pro-Union group that staged raids in Missouri before and during the Civil War.

Missouri Compromise An agreement made by the U.S. Congress in 1820 to admit Missouri into the Union as a slave state and Maine as a free state.

plateau A large, relatively flat area that stands above the surrounding land.

prairie A large area of level or gently rolling grassy land with few trees.

swamp A wetland permanently soaked with water. Woody plants (trees and shrubs) are the main form of vegetation.

tributary A river or stream that feeds, or flows into, a larger river.

Index

71

Acknowledgements:

Jim Hamilton, p. 2; Maryland Cartographics, Inc., pp. 2, 10; Jack Lindstrom, p. 6; Missouri Historical Society, pp. 7 (neg. #862), 20 (neg. #110a), 21 (J. N. Marchand, neg. #4a), 24 (neg. C-6a), 32–33; Ron Spomer / Visuals Unlimited, pp. 8–9; Jim Rathert / Missouri Department of Conservation, pp. 11, 12, 16, 47, 54 (full page), 55, 58 (right), 59, 60, 61; permission granted by the Missouri Division of Tourism, pp. 13, 15, 31, 42, 44 (right), 45, 46 (left), 49, 53, 54 (inset), 71; Richard Thom / Visuals Unlimited, pp. 17, 28, 52, 69; Cahokia Mounds State Historical Site, pp. 19, 44 (left); The Thomas Gilcrease Institute of American History and Art, Tulsa, Oklahoma, p. 23; Laura Westland, pp. 25, 30; Ohio Historical Society, p. 26; from the collections of the St. Louis Mercantile Library Association, pp. 27, 37; Kent & Donna Dannen, pp. 29, 36, 57; Library of Congress, pp. 34, 64 (bottom left); New Madrid Historical Museum, p. 35; University of Louisville, Kentucky, Ford Album Collection (neg. #77.1.314), p. 38; Missouri Department of Natural Resources, p. 39; Robert Tyszka ©, p. 40; Scott Rovak, St. Louis Cardinals, p. 46 (right); Chrysler Corporation, p. 48; Missouri Farm Bureau, pp. 50, 51; Len Rue, Jr. / Visuals Unlimited, p. 58 (left); State Historical Society of Missouri, pp. 62 (lower right, top, & bottom), 65 (lower right, bottom); Hollywood Book & Poster Co., pp. 62 (top left & right, bottom left), 64 (top left); National Baseball Hall of Fame and Museum, Inc., p. 63 (top right); Anheuser-Busch Corporate Archives, p. 63 (lower left); J. C. Penney Company, Inc., p. 63 (lower right); New York Public Library, Astor, Lenox and Tilden Foundations, p. 64 (upper right); Independent Picture Service, pp. 64 (bottom right), 65 (top); Dodd, Mead, and Co., Inc., p. 65 (bottom left); Hannibal Convention and Visitors Bureau, p. 65 (lower right, top); Jean Matheny, p. 66.